Cool Gets Hot

– GREGOR GIRVAN –

Cool Gets Hot

ISBN : 978-178456-762-0

First published 2021 by UPFRONT PUBLISHING
Peterborough, England.

An environmentally friendly book printed and bound in England
by www.printondemand-worldwide.com

Bear Words

groddle – human (man or woman)

grout – bad human

A New Day

The dressing room door flew open. An angry looking Cool stomped in and made his way to his locker. Wakey looked towards his pal and shouted over 'welcome back big pole, how was home?'

Cool had been back to northern Russia to spend time with his parents but the visit had clearly left him unhappy. He turned to Wakey and exclaimed 'Why don't groddles care about our planet, are they all turning into grouts?'

Seeing his friend agitated, Wakey wanted to help. 'Are your folks OK?' he asked gently.

'No, that's the problem' Cool replied.

'They've both lost a lot of weight and are very anxious' he continued but before he could explain, the conversation was interrupted by Luigi, the coach. 'This morning after warm up, we'll concentrate on free kicks' and he drew some sketches on the board to demonstrate the practice routines.

'We'll talk later' Wakey whispered to Cool.

The training session didn't go well for Cool. He missed several crosses and failed to stop a few shots he would usually have saved.

'Still on holiday?' Luigi asked.

'Sorry coach, I've had a lot on my mind' replied Cool. Luigi knew his keeper worked hard in training and usually performed well so he decided it was just a temporary lapse.

What To Do?

After showering, Wakey approached Cool. 'Fancy a drink?'

'If you're paying, how could I refuse?' Cool replied and the two pals set off to the local café where they ordered some juice and sat down opposite one another.

'So what happened?' asked Wakey.

'You know the ice floes are melting more than ever, well it means my parents have to travel much further to find food. And what's more they go into areas that groddles say belong to them' Cool explained.

'The result is that they don't get enough to eat, use up a lot of energy and end up being chased away from groddle-occupied land' he continued.

'But that's not fair, especially when groddles have caused the problem in the first place' exclaimed Wakey.

'Exactly' Cool replied. 'The animal kingdom didn't create global warming, it was groddles and their stuff' he said in a raised voice.

'We have to do something' Wakey suggested. 'But what, and who would listen?' asked Cool.

Wakey put his paws on his head and started to think.

Cool looked at his sloth bear friend. He thought Wakey needed a furcut and wondered how he'd look after using groddle curling tongs. Cool knew his pal was a good football player and very modest, making him popular with the other Bears.

'I know' Wakey suddenly exclaimed. 'You should meet up with Professor Coogasova.'

'But why?' asked Cool.

'So ... the Prof. is respected around the world because of her knowledge about environmental damage. She talks passionately but has difficulty getting groddles to change their ways. Maybe with your help she could make a difference. Groddles love football and you're one of the best known polar bears on the planet ... although it's a shame you can't catch a ball'.

Cool smiled back at his pal and made the decision to think carefully about Wakey's idea.

Cool Takes Action

Making his way home, Cool took a path through some fields and spotted some groddles in the back of a truck. Hiding behind some bushes, he watched in silence.

It soon became clear they were grouts. They were dumping all sorts of rubbish and broken things onto the land. Fuming with rage, Cool stared at the grouts and willed them to stop.

Out of nowhere, the grouts' bottoms began to expand like enormous balloons.

Cool started to laugh but covered his mouth so he wouldn't be heard while the two grouts looked at one another in horror as they wobbled on the spot.

In a panic, one of the grouts pulled his mobile phone from his pocket and made a call to the emergency services. Soon after, a groddle police car pulled up.

'What's happened here then?' asked the tall officer.

'We were offloading stuff and then our bums suddenly became huge; we can hardly move' exclaimed one of the grouts.

'OK, so you were illegally dumping waste?' the tall officer enquired.

'Well yes, but how can we get back to normal?' the other grout asked nervously.

'I don't know, but maybe first, we should roll you both to the police station' the officer suggested with a smirk on his face.

Cool had dealt with bumper bums before and decided to intervene. He walked over to the group, nodded to police officers and said 'Hi, maybe I can help get to the *bottom* of this'.

The grouts recognised Cool but weren't amused. The tall officer however replied 'Please, do go ahead.'

'Well, I've heard that if you repent for polluting and clean up, you can return to normal, but it only ever works once' Cool stressed.

The two grouts looked at one another and quickly apologised. Then, with much difficulty, they started picking up their discarded waste and loading it back in to the truck, dragging their vast, wobbly bottoms with them and working up quite a sweat whilst Cool and the officers looked on in amusement.

Quite exhausted, they sank to the ground and only then, to their great relief, did they realise that their normal bottoms were restored.

His work done, Cool decided it was time to make a move but before doing so he turned to the grouts 'remember, next time a big rear won't disappear.'

Professor Coogasova

The next morning, Cool decided to act on Wakey's suggestion and contact the Professor. He was in luck, the Professor could meet with him at 2pm.

Cool considered whether he should tell the Professor about his power to immobilise grouts who damage the environment. However, as telling groddle's anything could be risky, he decided against mentioning it.

Arriving at the university later in the day, Cool was shown to a meeting room and waited for the Professor to arrive. A few moments later the door opened and in walked a thin groddle. She had a typical flat face with groddle make up. Cool wondered why female groddles painted their eyes black, thinking perhaps that they wanted to look like pandas.

'Good afternoon, I'm Professor Coogasova' the groddle said with a beaming smile.

Cool smiled back, introduced himself and shook the groddle's hand.

After some general chat about the weather, which Cool knew groddles liked to talk about, he told the Professor about his parents. It was an issue with which the professor was very familiar. The Professor went on to talk about how much of the animal kingdom had been affected by climate change.

'But why don't groddles do something?' Cool asked in exasperation.

'The problem is that humans are aware of the problem and take small steps to help but aren't prepared to unite and take bigger steps.' the Professor replied.

She continued 'In footballing terms, what humans are doing to the planet, is like scoring an own goal. Until that message is fully understood, it will always be difficult to stop global warming.'

Cool thought carefully about what the Professor had said and spoke up 'How can I help?'

'Well you could give me your support at the next climate conference or join some action groups but I doubt if that would be enough. Maybe you or The Ready Bears could do something dramatic at a televised match, perhaps display a banner or something?' the Professor suggested as she scratched her head.

'Thanks' said Cool 'I'll think about what you've said' and shaking the professor's hand, he made for the door.

What's Happening?

Cool saw his parents in the distance. He ran towards them but they seemed to be getting smaller and smaller. All around the snow was melting and other polar bears were trying desperately to find food. Ugly groddles started to shout and hurl missiles at the bears but there was nowhere for them to run.

Cool approached the groddles and waved frantically at them to make them stop but it made no difference. A big groddle hurled a rock at Cool and he winced as it hit him on the shoulder. Another rock hit him on the head and he fell to the ground in pain. His mind was spinning as he despaired; 'What have bears done wrong?'

There was no answer. He saw grouts standing above him with clubs raised ... then darkness.

Cool sat up with a jerk. It had been a bad dream.

The Big Match Build-Up

The next day, on their way to training, Cool recounted his meeting with the Professor to Wakey and told him about his dream. He also revealed the power he had used on grouts.

Wakey's mouth dropped as he took in what Cool had said. He paused for a few moments and said 'You should do something to make an impact … but causing grouts to have bumper bottoms wouldn't be the answer. They have to want to change things themselves, groddledom has to take worldwide action'.

Cool looked at his shaggy friend and slowly replied 'You're right about the butts but how to make an impact … that's what I can't work out.'

They made their way to the training ground and settled into the dressing room to hear Luigi's team talk. Tactics were discussed and the coach reminded his players of the importance of the match. The Ready Bears had drawn 1 - 1 with the Barcelona Bruins away from home; so a win or a 0 - 0 draw would be enough to get them through to the final of the Continent Cup.

The team listened carefully but were suddenly interrupted by a loud trump. All the bears turned towards Jimmy who was trying to look innocent.

Luigi smiled, happy that the team had taken his comments on board and added:

'OK, it sounds as if a trumpeter has called the session to an end'.

As the players headed off, Luigi called over to Cool. The polar bear turned and walked over to the coach.

'How are you feeling?' asked Luigi.

'I'm fine ... and looking forward to keeping a clean sheet tomorrow' Cool replied confidently.

'The team's depending on you, I know you'll make an impact' Luigi added as he looked his goalkeeper in the eye.

'Nae problem' (no problem) Cool replied in a Scottish accent.

Luigi smiled; his keeper had been with The Ready Bears for 3 years and had mastered the local accent perfectly.

Match Day

The alarm clock sounded and Cool sprang out of bed. He'd slept well and was glad that it was nightmare free. During breakfast he thought about how he could make an impact when an idea sprang into his head.

Several hours later in the Blue Park dressing room, Cool called Wakey over. 'What's up big pole, feeling a bit nervous? ' Wakey asked.

'No, I'm fine but I need you to do something for me' Cool replied.

Leading Wakey through to the bathroom area, Cool picked up a tin of black paint and a brush. He rolled up his football jersey and turned his back to his shaggy friend.

'I got this paint from the store this morning. I want you to write something on my back with it' said Cool holding his jersey up.

'Oh I get it, you're going to take your shirt off at the end of the game and demonstrate how you feel. That should make the news' Wakey realised enthusiastically.

Cool smiled at his pal, standing quietly as Wakey applied the paint and waiting for it to dry. Then pulling his jersey down, the two pals headed off to join their team mates.

The Ready Bears ran onto the park and were greeted by a deafening noise from the packed stadium.

The match started at a frantic pace and The Ready Bears were soon on the defensive so Cool needed to make some great saves. At the end of the first half, the score remained 0 - 0.

In the second half, the team from Barcelona continued to have most of the possession and came close to scoring several times. Jock had a couple of long range shots but it was Cool who starred for The Ready Bears. The fans began to whistle as the game entered stoppage time. When Chi, the Bears captain, won a tackle he decided to pass the ball back to his keeper.

Cool trapped the ball with his feet and looked up. He knew a long kick up field would probably be the last of the game and The Ready Bears would go through to the final. However, he pulled up his shirt and did a complete turn to show the words on his back which revealed *OUR PLANET TOO*.

Players from both teams stopped and stared in amazement.

Cool turned towards the goal he had been defending, then slowly and calmly kicked the ball forward. There was complete silence in the ground as the ball rolled over the line and into the back of the net. A few moments later the referee's whistle blew, The Ready Bears had lost 1-0.

Cool started to walk towards the tunnel when he was joined by Wakey.

'That was mad but brave ...and I'm proud of you.' Wakey put his arm round his pal and they walked across the pitch together. Both bears were prepared for some abuse but to their surprise, a few fans started to clap, then more and then more again. Soon every groddle in the stadium was standing and clapping. The bears from both sides recognised what Cool had done and formed a guard of honour to cheer him off the field.

Luigi approached shaking his head but smiling at the same time. 'Not quite the impact I was expecting' he muttered.

The Aftermath

Just minutes after the match, Cool's actions were already headline news and all over social media.

One leading broadcaster reported THE GREATEST OWN GOAL, not what the Ready Bear's goalkeeper had done but what humans are doing to the planet.

It came as a surprise to Cool but from around the world, there was no criticism only recognition of his brave action. As the days passed, Cool was heartened to see more and more positive steps to protect the environment and cut global warming being planned.

An excited Professor Coogasova called Cool on his mobile. She had been invited to take part in a United World action group conference that was to be held in Glasgow, their home city.

Best of all, Cool's parents had been in touch and told him that the local groddles had stopped the attacks and were leaving food for them.

A couple of days later, Cool went for a run in the park and just through the gates, he noticed two groddles up ahead. They both had bumper bums … and had great difficulty moving. As he got closer, he recognised who they were.

They looked at Cool and were clearly glad to see him. 'Can you help us again?' one of the grouts pleaded.

'I'm sorry, no, you should have listened to my warning' Cool replied and walked slowly away. He was still optimistic about the future but wondered why some groddles never learn and become grouts.

Relaxing at home later that day, Cool drifted off to sleep. He saw images of bare ground where ice had been, forests burning, groddle settlements submerged by the sea .... and no bears anywhere.

The Club Code

✓ *Play fair, you're a Ready Bear*

✓ *Don't dive, cheats won't thrive*

✓ *Respect the ref. he's not deaf*

✓ *Don't waste time, it's a crime*